Magic Pony Carousel
Book 5

FLAME
THE DESERT PONY

Magic Pony Carousel
Book 5

FLAME
THE DESERT PONY

Poppy Shire

Illustrations by Ron Berg

HarperTrophy®

An Imprint of HarperCollins*Publishers*

★ ★ ★ ★ ★

FLAME THE DESERT PONY

Text copyright © 2008 by Working Partners

Illustrations copyright © 2008 by Ron Berg

All rights reserved. Printed in the United States of America.
No part of this book may be used or reproduced in any manner
whatsoever without written permission except in the case of brief
quotations embodied in critical articles and reviews. For informa-
tion address HarperCollins Children's Books, a division of
HarperCollins Publishers, 1350 Avenue of the Americas, New
York, NY 10019.

www.harpercollinschildrens.com

Library of Congress Cataloging-in-Publication Data is available.

ISBN 978-0-06-083794-5 (pbk.)

Typography by Sasha Illingworth

❖

First Edition

★ ★ ★ ★ ★

With special thanks to Gill Harvey

Chapter 1

The fairground looked lovely in the misty morning light. It was in Chloe's local park, at the bottom of a hill. She gazed down on the colorful rides in delight as she and her dad made their way to the entrance.

"Come on—let's find an exciting ride!" she cried as soon as they were inside the gates.

"Don't you want to get a hot dog first?" her dad asked.

Chloe loved hot dogs. She was about to say yes, but one of the rides suddenly caught her eye. She gasped.

"'Barker's Magic Pony Carousel,'" she read out loud.

The carousel was painted in red, gold, and silver swirls, and the beautiful wooden ponies moved gracefully up and down under rows of twinkling lights. Chloe couldn't tear her eyes away!

"Is that a no?" teased her dad.

"Do you think I could have a hot dog *after* trying the carousel?" Chloe said.

"Oh, I think so," her dad said. "Why don't you go and get on board? We can find a hot dog stand after you've had your ride."

"Thanks, Dad," Chloe said happily. She didn't have any brothers or sisters to play with, but her dad made sure that she never felt lonely. He was always taking her to do fun things, and at home they liked reading detective stories together.

She skipped over to the carousel to choose a

pony. The ride had just slowed to a halt, and one pony seemed to be gazing right at her. It was a stunning golden palomino with a creamy mane and tail and beautiful big brown eyes. From its pretty face with its slightly upturned nose, Chloe knew it must be an Arabian pony, and by the look of the saddle and bridle it could have come straight out of the desert!

She ran forward for a closer look. The pony's saddle was covered in deep ruby-red velvet with a golden fringe all the way around the edge. The matching ruby saddlecloth was embroidered with palm trees and birds in shiny gold thread. Red and gold tassels dangled from the edge, and there were matching tassels on the breastplate and bridle.

"Wow!" Chloe exclaimed. At her local riding school, she loved helping to get ponies ready for shows. She wasn't a very confident rider yet, but she was really good at braiding manes and weaving pretty ribbons into the hair. She looked closely at the gorgeous saddlecloth. Whoever had made this must love decorating ponies as much as she did!

"Hello there!" said a deep, friendly voice.

Chloe whirled around and saw a tall man stepping down from the carousel. He was wearing a red velvet suit lined with green silk and a stripy red and green top hat.

"Hello," said Chloe. "Are you Mr. Barker?"

"I am indeed!" said Mr. Barker, his eyes sparkling. "Would you like to ride on my splendid carousel?"

Chloe nodded. "Yes, please. I'd like to ride the palomino, if that's okay."

Mr. Barker stroked his chin. "Well, that's fine by me," he said, "but we'll have to see

what the carousel thinks."

"The carousel?" Chloe was puzzled.

Mr. Barker tapped his nose and leaned toward her. "It's a *magic* carousel, remember!" he whispered. Then he reached out and took a bright orange balloon from a passing balloon seller. With a flourish, he pulled a little pony-shaped badge out of his lapel. "Now, Chloe, let's see if your wish can come true!"

Before Chloe had time to wonder how Mr. Barker could possibly know her name, he burst the balloon with the badge pin. *POP!* Chloe stared in amazement as a little pink ticket fluttered to the ground.

Mr. Barker beamed at her. "I think you'll find there's something written on it," he said.

Chloe could just see some swirly silver writing on one side of the ticket. She bent down to pick it up. "'Flame,'" she read, then looked up at Mr. Barker.

"What a coincidence!" he said with a wink.

Chloe ran over to the palomino. There was a name written on the pretty red headband. She stood on tiptoe to read it.

"'Flame'!" she exclaimed.

Chapter 2

"All aboard!" cried Mr. Barker. "Step up, step up for the most exciting ride of your lives! The Magic Pony Carousel is about to start!"

Quickly Chloe scrambled up onto Flame's back. She had read books about different kinds of ponies, and she knew Arabians came from the desert, where they had to be strong and fast to race long distances over the sand.

She patted Flame's shiny wooden neck, then held on tight to the twisty golden pole. The carousel began to turn, moving her gently up and down. Chloe thought about what it would be like to ride across the desert with the sun beating down. She could almost feel the warm rays on her skin . . . but then the air began to shimmer, and Chloe saw swirls of pink glitter falling around her. She rubbed her eyes. She must be imagining things! But no—the glitter was still falling softly.

"Ow!" she exclaimed, as specks flew into her face. "What's that?"

She looked down and saw grains of sand dusting the pommel of the saddle. "Sand?" she muttered, brushing it away with her hand. "I can't be imagining *that*!"

The glitter began to clear, and she tried to grab the twisty golden pole again—but it had disappeared! Instead, her hands landed on a soft, silky mane. Chloe nearly fell out of the saddle in surprise. Hastily she steadied herself on the saddle's high pommel and picked up the red leather reins. What was going on? She wasn't sitting on a carousel at all now. Flame was a real, live pony!

The fairground had vanished. Instead, there was golden, shimmering sand as far as she could see. She and Flame were galloping between the rolling dunes of a desert.

"Steady!" cried Chloe. She had never ridden this fast before! She gave a little tug on the reins and Flame slowed down to a canter. But the sand was still flying into her face, so Chloe pulled on the reins again, slowing the pony to a trot. She groped for the pocket of her fleecy pink cardigan, looking for a tissue to hold over her nose. To her astonishment, the pocket wasn't there. She glanced down. She wasn't wearing her cardigan at all!

Chloe was wearing a pale blue cotton gown

embroidered with pretty yellow cross stitches. There was a little kerchief around her neck in rich sky blue, decorated with a fringe of tiny red and blue beads. Chloe quickly lifted it up to cover her nose and mouth. It would keep the sand out perfectly. Then she reached up and patted her hair. Phew! She was still wearing her favorite barrette decorated with rainbow-colored butterflies. This was all very mysterious but exciting, too!

As Flame's hooves thudded across the golden sand, Chloe saw that they were approaching a little town. All the houses were whitewashed, and many of them had domed roofs that stood out against the blue sky. In the brilliant sunshine, they were almost too bright to look at. Chloe shaded her eyes with one hand as Flame reached the edge of the town.

They trotted down a narrow street, and Chloe

spotted a man leading a donkey laden with baskets of vegetables. She reined Flame to a walk and followed the donkey over the smooth cobbles. The street opened into a square with palm trees in the middle, surrounding a stone well. All around the edge of the square were colorful, busy market stalls.

"Wow!" said Chloe. "What a great place!"

"Yes, isn't it?" agreed a soft voice.

Chloe looked around, wondering who had spoken. There wasn't anyone nearby. With a shrug, she nudged Flame forward, looking at the different market stalls. There were richly woven rugs and hangings, mounds of scented spices, wonderful fabrics, and clothes.

"Figs! Lovely plump figs!" called one stall owner. He smiled at Chloe and held one out to her.

She laughed and shook her head. The fig

looked delicious, but she didn't have any money.

A woman wearing a bright red shawl walked past with a pail of water balanced on her head. The sight of the crystal-clear water made Chloe realize how thirsty she was.

"Oh! I'd love a drink," she exclaimed out loud.

"So would I!"

It was the mysterious voice again! Chloe peered around, but no one seemed to be taking any notice of her. Shaking her head, she slipped down from Flame's back and led the pony over to the palm trees beside the well. She tied Flame's reins to a wooden post.

"I won't be a minute, Flame," she said, patting the pony's neck. Then she headed toward the well. A group of girls was waiting with stone jars for their turn to draw water.

"Hey!" called the voice again.

Chloe spun around. There was no one behind her, just Flame tied to the post.

"Please could I have a drink, too?" begged the voice. "It was very hot galloping across the desert!"

Chloe stared hard. Could it be . . . ? She stepped forward. "Flame," she whispered. "Was that you?"

The palomino blinked her big brown eyes. "Of course it was!" she said.

Chloe flung her arms around her neck. "You can talk!" she cried. "This is the best carousel ride ever!"

Flame nuzzled Chloe's cheek. "I can talk, but the ticket you picked with my name on it means that only you will be able to understand me," she said. "The carousel has sent us here to help someone and solve a problem. I'm not sure what it is, though. We'll have to find that out for ourselves."

Chloe had a worrying thought. "What about my dad? He won't know where I've gone!"

Flame shook her long silky mane. "Don't worry," she said. "When we get back, it will be as if we've never been away."

"Wow!" breathed Chloe. "My very own magical adventure with my very own Arabian pony!"

"That's right," agreed Flame. "A very *thirsty* Arabian pony!"

Chapter 3

Chloe untied the reins and led Flame over to the well. She smiled shyly at the girls. Three of them were chatting together, and they smiled back. But the fourth girl didn't look up from filling her water jar. They all wore colorful gowns like the one Chloe was wearing. She loved the bright orange gown worn by the girl closest to her.

An elderly woman finished filling her jar and offered Chloe a chance to use the bucket that had to be lowered into the well. Chloe pushed it over the edge of the stone wall and listened to it splash into the water below. Then she pulled on the rope. Slowly the bucket came up, full of sparkling water. She began to pull the bucket over the side of the well, but it was heavier than she expected. The bucket slipped from her fingers, and sloshed cold water all over the girl in the beautiful orange gown!

"Oh!" gasped the girl.

"I'm so sorry!" Chloe exclaimed.

But the girl was laughing. She had warm brown eyes and long dark hair with coppery highlights that gleamed in the sun. "Don't worry." she said. "It's nice and cool!"

She helped Chloe put the bucket on the ground. As she bent down, the girl dipped the tips of her fingers into the bucket and flicked water over Chloe's hair.

Chloe shook her head and felt drops of cool water trickle down her neck. Then she reached

into the bucket and splashed the girl back! The girl yelped and began to run around the well. Laughing, Chloe chased after her new friend until she dived behind two of the other girls.

"Come on, you two, protect me!" she begged, peeping out from between them as Chloe approached.

"You're joking, Mina!" they exclaimed. One of them reached into her own bucket and flicked more water over Mina's orange gown. Mina squealed and ran off again. The other girls helped Chloe chase her. They were soon gasping with laughter.

"Come on, Hanna, help me!" Mina called to the fourth girl.

Hanna smiled but shook her head and stayed next to the well.

Mina tried to hide behind Flame.

The pony stuck her nose into the bucket of

water. "Watch this," she said to Chloe.

As Mina crept forward to peep under Flame's neck, the pony suddenly lifted her head out of the bucket, splashing *all* the girls, even Chloe.

"Flame!" Chloe squealed. "You weren't supposed to get me, too. I'm *soaked*!"

Flame snorted and looked around with wide, innocent eyes.

Mina laughed. "She meant to do it—I'm sure she did!"

Chloe put her arm around Flame's neck and smiled at her new friends. "This is Flame," she said. "And I'm Chloe. Do you have ponies, too?"

Mina nodded. "Yes, but she's at home in her stable. Her name's Flicker, and I'm Mina."

"I'm Amira, and this is my sister Nadia," said another of the girls. She picked up her water jar. "We'd better get going, Nadia."

"Okay," said Nadia. "Nice to meet you, Chloe."

Mina waved as they walked out of the square, then turned to the fourth girl, who was still standing beside the well. "This is my best friend, Hanna," she told Chloe.

Chloe watched as Hanna balanced her water jar on top of her head and walked gracefully toward them. "I'm going home," Hanna said. "Are you coming?"

"I just wanted you to meet my new friend Chloe," said Mina.

Hanna glanced at Chloe and Flame but looked away again without smiling. "Another new friend, Mina? I have to go. My mom's waiting for me," she said coolly. "Are you coming or not?"

Mina hesitated. Chloe hoped she would stay by the well. She liked Mina a lot, and she didn't know anyone else here.

Mina picked up her water jar. "I haven't filled my jar yet," she said. "I'll catch up with you at your house."

Hanna gave a shrug and walked off. Chloe thought she was acting very oddly. Mina was so friendly, but Hanna didn't seem friendly at all!

"Maybe she was feeling left out," Flame whispered in Chloe's ear.

Chloe stroked her neck and nodded. That might make sense.

"Bye, Hanna!" called Mina, but her friend didn't turn around.

Mina's face fell, and Chloe felt sorry for her. But then Mina grinned. "I think Hanna needs her ears tested," she joked. "Never mind. I'll see her later. Let's take this water home and you can meet Flicker."

Chloe watched as Mina filled her water jar, then balanced it on top of her head. "How do you do that?" she asked.

Mina looked puzzled. "I don't know. I've always done it—all the girls here carry things on their heads. Why, don't you?"

Chloe felt her cheeks grow hot. How could she explain that she'd arrived by magic? "Um . . ." she began.

"Tell her we're from a different village," suggested Flame.

"We don't do that in my village," Chloe said quickly, patting Flame's neck. It was wonderful having a secret friend to help her out!

"Really?" said Mina, leading the way across the square. "Have you come for the pageant?"

"The pageant? Oh—yes," Chloe stuttered. Whatever the pageant was, it sounded fun. And it obviously gave her a good reason to be visiting the town!

"I thought you must have," said Mina.

"Flame has such a gorgeous saddlecloth. Did you make it yourself?"

"No. I wish I had, though," Chloe answered truthfully. She was beginning to wonder how long she'd be able to answer all Mina's questions without admitting where she'd come from!

"Try changing the subject," whispered Flame, coming to her rescue again.

But then, to Chloe's relief, Mina was distracted by one of the stall owners. She seemed to know everyone! All the people were very friendly. They patted Flame's neck as Chloe led her behind Mina. Chloe thought Flame looked pleased to be getting so much attention.

Mina turned down another street and then another. There were chickens pecking in the dirt, and sometimes a goat stood tethered to a ring in the wall. People left their doors wide open, and Chloe peeked in as they passed. Inside the shadowy houses, chatting women sat cross-legged on colorful mats. The men seemed to prefer sitting outside, gathering at street corners to drink little glasses of black tea.

"It's not far now," said Mina. "I can't wait to show you my saddlecloth. I've been working on it for days!"

"You've made your own?" exclaimed Chloe. "What color is it?"

"Bright blue silk," said Mina proudly, "with lots of gold and silver stitching."

"That sounds lovely," said Chloe.

Mina flashed her a smile. "It's almost finished—I've just got a tiny bit of stitching left to do. I don't have any brothers or sisters, so Hanna's been helping me to finish it."

Chloe knew exactly what it felt like, being an only child. "I don't have any brothers or sisters either," she admitted. "But friends are just as good!"

Mina nodded. "That's what I think, too." Then her face clouded over and she frowned. "But it's odd. Hanna's been grumpy lately," she said. "I know she's shy, but she's not usually this quiet. I can't figure out what's wrong."

Chloe didn't know what to say. Hanna hadn't been very friendly toward her, but she was still Mina's best friend!

Mina turned one more corner, and then pointed to a house at the end of the street. "That's where I live," she said. "And there's the stable next to it."

The house was so pretty! Its mud-brick walls were whitewashed, and a beautiful dome formed part of the roof. They entered a courtyard through an archway with patterns cut around the edge of the mud brick. Bright pink flowers were growing around the arch.

Mina put the water jar down next to a doorway.

"I'm home!" she called into the house, before leading the way across the courtyard to the stable. "I expect Flame's tired," Mina said. "She can rest in the stall next to Flicker for a while."

"That sounds like a good idea!" Flame whispered in Chloe's ear. "Mina could be the person we're supposed to help. The stable might give us some clues."

Chloe stroked her soft nose and straightened her creamy gold forelock. "Maybe there'll be some nice hay, too," she whispered back.

Mina opened the stable door and was greeted with a friendly whinny. "Hello, Flicker!" she said to a pretty chestnut pony. "Say hello to Flame!"

Chloe led Flame into the stall and slipped her bridle off. The ponies looked at each other with their ears pricked, then touched noses and blew softly at each other.

"They're going to get on perfectly!" Mina laughed. "Come on, let's go to the tack room. I'm *dying* to show you my saddlecloth!"

She skipped through another doorway, with Chloe close behind her. But the moment she stepped inside the tack room, Mina let out a wail.

"Oh no!" she cried. "It's *ruined*!"

Chapter 4

"What's happened?" Chloe asked. She peered over Mina's shoulder. A square of blue silk was lying crumpled on the floor.

Mina stepped forward and picked it up.

"Look!" she sobbed. "Someone's completely wrecked it!"

Chloe stared at the saddlecloth in dismay. The blue cloth was covered in mud and dust, and there were rips and tears all over the fabric. Worst of all, the beautiful silver and gold embroidery was all picked loose.

"How *awful*," Chloe said. "Who would do something so horrible?"

"I don't know." Mina hiccupped. "But there's no way I'll be able to join the pageant now."

Chloe put an arm around her. Surely there was something she could do to help.

"Could you help her make another one, Chloe?" called Flame, who was watching through the door.

Chloe stared at the ruined saddlecloth. It might just be possible. "Mina, when's the pageant?" she asked.

"Tomorrow afternoon." Mina sniffed. "It's too late to do anything now."

Chloe shook her head. "No, it isn't," she said. "I can sew, too. If we both work really hard, we could make a new one. Where did you buy the cloth and the thread?"

"The market," Mina said, sounding more

hopeful. "It'll be closing soon, though . . ."

"But it's still open now, isn't it?" said Chloe.
Mina nodded.

"Then wait here," Chloe ordered. She ran back into the stable and took Flame's bridle off its hook. Hurriedly, she slipped it over the pony's ears. "I think I've found the problem!" she whispered. "I need to help Mina make a new saddlecloth. Can you remember the way back to the market?"

"Of course I can!" said Flame, tossing her head. "Let's go!"

Chloe scrambled up onto her back, and Flame trotted out of the courtyard.

"We won't be long!" Chloe called over her shoulder to Mina.

Flame set off along the winding streets. Chloe clung on to the saddle—with all the twisting and turning, she was worried she'd fall off!

"Just sit up nice and straight," said Flame. "Don't lean forward too much. Then you won't need to hold on so tight."

Chloe tried to do as Flame said, but it was difficult to think about riding *and* where they were going. She was glad Flame had such a good sense of direction, because she soon felt completely lost.

"Look—there's a tea glass on the ground. That's where those men were drinking tea," Flame puffed, and turned right.

Chloe caught a glimpse of the glass as they cantered past.

"And there's one of the goats we passed before," said the palomino, pointing her nose to where a black-and-white goat was tethered. "We're almost there!"

"Well done, Flame!" Chloe gasped as they clattered into the market square. "You're amazing.

Now all we have to do is find the fabric stall."

Some of the stall owners were packing up. "Oh *please* let the fabric stall still be here!" Chloe pleaded out loud.

"Are you looking for me?" called a cheerful voice. Chloe twisted around in the saddle—and there was a stall overflowing with beautiful fabrics! There were rolls of cloth in all colors of the rainbow—bright reds and yellows, brilliant greens and deep, luscious purples.

Chloe slid down from the saddle. "I'm so glad I've found you!" she exclaimed. "My friend Mina bought her fabric and threads from you to make her saddlecloth. But now it's been ruined and we have to make another one in double-quick time. The only trouble is, I'm not even sure which fabric she bought . . ." she finished, looking hopefully at the stall owner.

The man smiled. He had lovely sparkling

eyes. He looked just like Mr. Barker from the Magic Pony Carousel!

"Oh yes, I know Mina," he said. "And I remember what she bought, too." He started lifting several rolls of fabric out of the way. "Now, where is it?" he muttered. "Ah! I think it was this one." He pulled out a roll of silky blue fabric.

"That's right!" Chloe said.

"She used this to make it soft for Flicker's back," he went on, pulling out a roll of thick gray-blue felt, "and this thread." He pulled a box from underneath the stall and picked out a spool of silver thread. Then he scratched his head. "Now, where's that gold thread?"

Chloe watched as he hunted for the gold thread. At last, the stall owner shook his head and held up an empty spool. "I'm sorry. I've sold it all, I'm afraid," he said.

"Oh dear," said Chloe. The saddlecloth

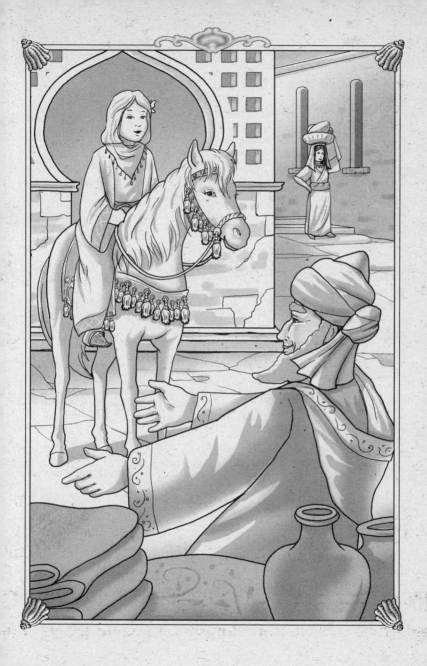

wouldn't be the same without the gold!

"I have plenty of green and blue thread," the stall owner offered.

Chloe shook her head. Those colors wouldn't show up very well on the blue fabric. "Never mind," she said. "The blue cloth and silver thread will have to do."

She watched as he wrapped them in paper, while trying not to feel too disappointed about the gold thread.

"The silver will look lovely on its own," whispered Flame reassuringly.

Suddenly Chloe's heart skipped a beat. How could she have been so silly? She didn't have any money! She'd left Mina in such a hurry that she'd forgotten to ask for some. *Now* what was she going to do?

The stall owner handed her the parcel. "I—I'm sorry," Chloe stammered. "I've made a horrible mistake. . . . You see I don't have any . . ."

The man smiled, looking more like Mr. Barker than ever. "Now, don't you worry," he said. "I know Mina's family very well. They can pay me tomorrow."

Chloe breathed a big sigh of relief. "Thank you!" she cried. She took the parcel and turned to climb back into the saddle.

"Wait a minute," said the man. "Before you go, there's one more thing. . . ." He held up a little bag. "I'm sure you can think of something to do with these."

Chloe peeped into the bag. It was full of silk ribbons, all in different colors. "They're perfect!" she cried. "I'll be able to weave them into Flame and Flicker's manes, just like I do at the riding school!"

"I thought you'd find them useful," said the stall owner with a wink.

Chloe climbed back into the saddle and waved good-bye.

Flame set off at a canter, and Chloe held the reins in one hand, clasping her parcels tight with the other.

"Good luck!" the man called after her.

Chapter 5

"You're sitting much better now!" said Flame, as they clattered along the little streets.

"Do you think so?" Chloe was delighted.

"Yes. Just try to keep your lower legs still," Flame told her.

Chloe nodded and concentrated on her riding. Flame was the best riding instructor she'd ever had! But then, as they drew closer to Mina's house, she began to feel worried. "What if Mina's really upset about the gold thread?" she wondered. "She might not want to make a saddlecloth without it."

"Well, we've done our best," said Flame. "The silver will look nice."

"But she was so proud of all that gold stitching," Chloe said sadly.

Flame slowed to a trot as they turned the corner into Mina's street. Suddenly she stopped dead.

"What is it?" Chloe asked in alarm.

"I have an idea!" Flame whinnied. "You could use some strands of my tail instead of gold thread. They look very shiny in the sun."

"That's a brilliant idea!" Chloe leaned down and hugged the pony's neck. "You're so clever, Flame. Come on, let's tell Mina!"

They found Mina sitting in the courtyard with the saddlecloth in her lap, picking at the ruined stitches. She looked up as Flame and Chloe rode in.

"Did you get everything?" she asked.

Chloe slid down to the ground and showed Mina the bag of fabrics and thread. "*Nearly* everything," she said. "There wasn't any gold thread left."

Mina's face fell. "No gold thread!"

"But I've got an idea," Chloe went on. She knew she had to pretend it was her own idea— Mina would never believe she had a talking pony! "We could use some hairs from Flame's tail instead."

Mina looked at Flame's flowing golden tail and smiled. She stood up and planted a kiss on Flame's soft muzzle. "Let's get started at once. My mom's given us a picnic dinner so that we can stay in the stable to make the new saddle-cloth. Look!" She picked up a basket made of different colored reeds.

It reminded Chloe of the bag she had. "And

look what the stall owner gave me, too!" She pulled out a handful of slippery ribbons to show Mina. "I can weave them into our ponies' manes."

"Perfect," said Mina. "Everything's going to be all right, isn't it?"

"Of course it is!" Chloe agreed.

The two girls took everything into the stable, then settled Flame next to Flicker. Mina shooed her fluffy black cat out of the hay store so they could each make a soft pile to sit on. The cat watched them, licking its paws, as they snuggled into the hay and started work. It was such a cozy place to be that it didn't feel like work at all! First, they embroidered the silk. Then they stitched the silk onto the felt underside, and Mina explained how she'd made pretty patterns with the thread.

"Let's do the silver part first," she said. "We

can weave the golden parts in afterward, with strands of Flame's tail."

"All right," Chloe said. "I'll start at the opposite end so we meet in the middle." Chloe's grandma had taught Chloe how to embroider last summer.

The girls worked in silence, concentrating hard. After a while, Mina looked up. "Are you hungry yet?" she asked.

Just then, Chloe's tummy rumbled, and they both laughed.

"I think that's a yes!" said Mina. "Here, have some bread. My mom makes it herself. And here's hummus to dip it in, and baba ghanoush—that's made with eggplant—and there's some cold lamb, too."

The two girls quickly finished their meal and filled the rack in the stable with fresh hay so their ponies could have supper, too. Then they went back to the sewing. Soon it began to get dark, and Mina fetched oil lamps. They made the stable look really pretty, casting a gentle orangey-yellow glow on the walls. Chloe looked at Flame, who had finished her hay and was dozing with her weight on three legs and one hoof tipped. Her golden coat looked beautiful in the soft lamplight.

The saddlecloth was beginning to take shape, though there was a lot of stitching to do. Once the silver thread was used up, Mina handed Chloe her sewing scissors, and she went over to Flame to cut some of her golden tail hairs.

Chloe ran back to Mina and showed her the hairs from Flame's tail. They shone in the lamp-light, exactly like gold.

"They're beautiful," Mina said. She threaded one through her needle. "I think I'll do a bird first," she said.

Chloe threaded her own needle and joined in.

At last, Mina sewed the final stitch—the top of a golden palm tree—and held up the cloth.

"Wow!" Chloe whispered. "I can't believe I've helped to make something so beautiful!"

Mina gave her a hug. "Well, you did," she said happily. She placed the saddlecloth safely to one side and sank back onto the hay.

Chloe yawned, stretching her arms above her head.

"I suppose we should go back into the house," Mina said sleepily, "but it's so comfortable here. . . ."

"I think I'm too tired to move," Chloe muttered. She felt her eyes closing . . . closing . . . She wriggled deeper into the soft warm hay and fell fast asleep.

She woke up with a jolt. The lamps were still burning, and it was very dark outside. Mina was asleep beside her, curled up on the hay. Chloe sat up. Something had woken her up. She listened carefully, her heart beating faster. Yes—there it was again! A soft noise just outside the stable.

"Flame!" she whispered, and the palomino twitched her ear to show she was awake. "Did you hear that? It sounded like footsteps."

Flame snorted. "I think I heard something," she said. She pricked her ears, listening. "It's stopped now. Don't worry, I'll keep one ear open. You can go back to sleep."

Chloe lay back on the hay. She wondered what she could have heard. Perhaps it was Mina's mom or dad, checking that they were okay. Or perhaps it had been nothing at all. She rested her head on her arm and soon fell back to sleep.

"Wake up, wake up!" called Mina's voice. "It's time for breakfast!"

Mina was shaking Chloe by the shoulder. She opened her eyes. Daylight was streaming into the stable and Flame and Flicker were munching a fresh batch of hay.

"It's pageant day!" Mina sang. "Come on. I bet my mom has cooked a delicious breakfast for us. She always does on pageant day!"

Chloe rubbed her eyes. "That sounds great," she said, scrambling to her feet. "How does the saddlecloth look in daylight?"

Mina's eyes lit up. "It's *gorgeous*," she declared, holding it up.

She was right. Sunbeams danced over the silver thread and the golden strands of Flame's tail, making them glint and sparkle.

Mina put the saddlecloth down and tried to open the stable door. But it didn't move. "That's funny," she said. "It never usually sticks!" She gave it another push. It *still* wouldn't move!

"Let me try," said Chloe. She leaned against the door and pushed with all her strength. The door didn't budge one tiny bit.

"It must be locked," Mina said in dismay. "Someone's locked it from the outside!"

"That must have been what we heard in the night, Chloe," said Flame, who was standing behind them. "You thought it was footsteps, didn't you?"

Chloe frowned. It was hard to believe that someone would lock them in. "Could it have happened by accident?" she asked Mina.

Mina shook her head. "You have to push the bolt across. What's going on, Chloe? First my saddlecloth was ruined, and now this!"

"I'm sure there must be an explanation," said Chloe. She wondered if she should tell Mina about the footsteps, but Mina seemed worried enough already. She ran her hand over her hair, trying to think of something that might help. Her hand brushed against her butterfly barrette.

"Could you use your barrette to unbolt the door?" Flame asked, watching her.

Chloe caught her eye and nodded. It was worth a try. She pulled the barrette out of her hair. "I could try sliding the bolt open with this," she said to Mina.

Mina frowned. "How?" she said. "The bolt's on the outside."

Chloe inspected the door. "Look, there's a little gap between the door and the frame. I can just see the knob of the bolt. I should be able to slide the barrette through it and push against the knob. It will slide the bolt back."

She opened the barrette and pushed the silver part through the gap. Then she wiggled it around until she could feel the side of the knob.

Mina peered anxiously over Chloe's shoulder.

"Is the bolt moving?"

Chloe wiggled the barrette some more. "Yes! I just felt it slide back a little bit!"

"Keep going!" Mina said.

With a final twist of the barrette, the bolt slid back and the door swung open. "Hurray!" Chloe shouted. "We did it!"

"*You* did it," Mina corrected her, giving her a hug. "I don't know what I would have done without you!" Then her face grew serious. "But we still don't know why these horrible things have happened." She shook her head. "Why would someone want to stop me from taking part in the pageant?"

Chapter 6

"Whoever is doing these things, we'll find him," Chloe promised. "Maybe we should go for a ride after breakfast to look for suspects."

Mina nodded. "Good idea," she said. "Come on. Let's have breakfast, then go and find Hanna. She loves detective stories. She'll help us to track the culprit down!"

"I love detective stories, too!" Chloe exclaimed. It was nice to find out that she and Hanna had something in common. It might make it easier to get to know her.

As soon as they had finished eating, they headed out to the stables to tack up the ponies. Flicker looked so pretty with her new saddle-cloth. The blue silk and gold and silver embroidery gleamed against her chestnut coat.

Chloe put on Flame's saddle and bridle and led her out of the stable. She stopped dead in the doorway.

"What is it?" Chloe whispered.

Flame scraped her hoof on the ground. "Look down there," she said.

Chloe frowned. Flame was pointing at some sunflower seeds scattered on the ground by the door.

"Well spotted, Flame," she whispered. She turned to Mina. "Mina, do you ever feed Flicker sunflower seeds?"

"No," said Mina. "Why?"

"There are some on the ground here. I don't

remember seeing them yesterday. They must have been dropped by the person who locked the stable door!"

Mina stared. "That's a great clue!" she said, her cheeks turning pink with excitement. "All we have to do is find someone who's been eating sunflower seeds!"

"It would be a good start," Chloe agreed. She patted Flame's neck gratefully.

The two girls mounted their ponies and trotted out of the yard. "Hanna lives in the next street," said Mina.

But when they got to Hanna's house, her mother told them that Hanna had gone for a ride in the desert with her brother.

"I know where they'll have gone," said Mina. "It won't take us long to catch up. We can gallop through the dunes."

Chloe felt a bit nervous. She remembered

how fast Flame had been galloping when they arrived from the carousel. Just from looking at Mina in the saddle, Chloe could tell that she was a much better rider. She hoped she'd be able to keep up without falling off!

"You won't go *too* fast, will you, Flame?" she whispered.

"You'll be fine," said Flame with a chuckle. "I'll tell you what to do."

Mina led the way to the edge of the town. In the distance were the rolling sand dunes. These dunes were higher than the ones Chloe had seen before, all different shades of yellow, gold, and orange, sculpted into gentle waves by the wind.

"Let's go!" Mina cried. Flicker gave a playful buck before leaping into a gallop, his heels kicking up the soft sand.

Chloe grabbed the pommel of her saddle in case Flame bucked, too!

"I won't buck," Flame called. "Just sit nice and still and let your hips rock in time to my movement."

Then she tossed her head and galloped after Flicker. Soon she was going faster than Chloe had ever been in her life. She twisted her fingers in Flame's mane and clung on tightly.

"You don't need . . . to grip so tight," Flame puffed. "You won't . . . fall off. Just . . . relax. Put your weight . . . into your stirrups."

Chloe did as she said, and to her surprise, she found that she felt much safer in the saddle. She laughed out loud as the wind whipped through her hair and sand flew up around her. She remembered her blue kerchief and pulled it up over her mouth to keep out the gritty sand.

The girls raced side by side until a little clump of palm trees came into sight. There were two other ponies there already, one gray and one black.

Mina slowed Flicker to a canter, and then a trot. "That's Hanna and her pony, Ebony," she said to Chloe, "and Hanna's brother Abdou with Cloud."

As they got closer, Chloe saw that the black pony had a pretty white blaze. Hanna was standing beside him, holding his bridle. Chloe slowed Flame to a walk behind Flicker, and they made their way around the clump of palm trees. A young boy was holding the gray pony's reins. When he saw Mina, he handed the reins to Hanna and ran toward them with a big smile.

"Hi, Mina!" he called. "Are you ready for the pageant?"

Mina stopped and smiled at the boy. "Hi, Abdou," she said. She swiveled around in her saddle to look back at Chloe. "This is Hanna's little brother. Abdou, this is my friend Chloe."

Abdou fished in his pocket. "Hello, Chloe,"

he said. He pulled out a packet of sunflower seeds and held it up to her. "Would you like some sunflower seeds?"

"Where did you get those?" Mina gasped.

Abdou looked puzzled. "Hanna gave them to me," he said. "She bought them in the market yesterday."

Chloe stared at Mina in dismay. Surely *Hanna* couldn't be the culprit! "Er, thanks, Abdou," Chloe said. "You keep the seeds for yourself. We've just had breakfast."

As they rode on toward Hanna, Chloe hoped that they were wrong. "Surely Mina's best friend couldn't do such horrible things to her!" she whispered to Flame.

Flame twitched one ear. "If she did, I expect she had a reason," she said.

Chloe followed as Mina slid down from Flicker's back and led her toward the black pony.

"Hello, Hanna," Mina said, sounding slightly nervous. "I thought we'd find you here."

Hanna shrugged. "I'm surprised you bothered looking for me," she said. "You didn't come over last night, even though you said you would."

"I'm sorry, Hanna," Mina said, looking very upset. "When I got home we found that my saddlecloth had been ruined. So we had to spend hours and hours making another one. And then someone locked us in the stable!"

Hanna looked at the ground and said nothing.

"We wanted you to help us find out who did it," Mina went on. "We found sunflower seeds outside the stable . . . but then . . . we just met Abdou and he was eating a packet of them and he said . . ." She trailed off.

When Hanna looked up, her eyes were full of tears. "I didn't touch your saddlecloth!" she burst out. "I promise I didn't!"

"I didn't say you did," Mina said in surprise. Flame nudged her arm and whickered, and Chloe guessed she was trying to get Mina to stay quiet. Hanna still had more to say.

A tear rolled down Hanna's cheek. "I didn't spoil your saddlecloth, but I locked you in the stable. I came over to find you last night, and I brought the sunflower seeds as a present. But you and Chloe were asleep on the hay. I was so jealous . . ." She scrubbed her face with the back of her hand. "So I locked the door and went away again."

Mina looked bewildered. "Jealous of what?" she said.

"You and Chloe, of course!" said Hanna. "You're always making new friends! Nadia and Amira play with us all the time, and now Chloe, too. Sometimes I think you don't like me at all."

Mina threw her arms around her friend. "Of course I like you!"

"I don't know why." Hanna sniffed. "I'm too shy to make friends the way you do. I end up feeling left out all the time."

Mina looked amazed.

"You were right, Flame," Chloe whispered. "You thought she might be feeling left out."

"Yes," the pony agreed. "I don't think she meant any real harm. She's obviously very sorry about locking the stable door."

Chloe stepped forward. "Mina told me that you like detective stories, Hanna. We still don't know who ruined her saddlecloth. Will you help us to find out?"

Hanna hesitated. "You mean you don't mind about the door?"

"Let's forget about it," Mina said. "Chloe got us out with her lucky barrette. But you won't do anything like that again, will you?"

"Of course not," Hanna said.

"Well then, that's fine," said Mina, linking her arm through her friend's. "We'll always be best friends, I promise."

Hanna smiled. "Good," she said. "I'm really sorry about the door." She turned to Chloe. "I'm glad you had your lucky barrette with you."

Chloe smiled back.

"Come on," said Mina. "We'd better get back into town if we're going to find out who *really* ruined my saddlecloth!"

Chapter 7

The girls trotted back across the dunes with Abdou and Cloud following them. They were trying to figure how to discover the culprit.

"Maybe there are some clues on the saddle-cloth," Hanna suggested.

"Clues?" Mina echoed. "It's totally ruined. How could there be any clues?"

But Chloe agreed with Hanna. "Detectives look for tiny traces of evidence," she said, stroking Flame's soft neck and thinking of the sunflower seeds. "I think Hanna's right. We should take a closer look at it!"

"I guess so," Mina said thoughtfully.

They made their way to Mina's house and took the ponies into the stable, where they showed Hanna the ruined saddlecloth.

Hanna frowned. "It doesn't look as though the threads have been cut," she said, turning the cloth over in her hands. "It looks as if they've been scratched or picked loose with something sharp."

Chloe peered over her shoulder. "And are those black hairs clinging to the silk?" She pointed.

Mina looked at Hanna. "That's definitely a clue! Who do we know with short black hair?"

Chloe inspected the hairs more closely. "I don't think these are human hairs," she said. "But I think I know what they are. . . ."

"*Cat* hairs!" Hanna exclaimed. "Of course!"

Suddenly Flame gave a whinny, and Chloe turned to see what she wanted. Mina's black cat was curled up in the hay rack, fast asleep.

"Let's have a look at his claws," said Chloe. "There could be evidence on them!"

She stroked the cat's head and then picked him up. Hanna took hold of his front paws and peered at them. "Look!" she said. "There are tiny bits of silver thread caught in the claws!"

"Pasha, you *naughty* cat!" Mina scolded.

Pasha gave a loud meow and wriggled out of Chloe's hands. Then he scampered out of the stable with his tail held high.

Mina smiled broadly. "I know Pasha didn't mean to upset me," she said. She gave Hanna a hug, then Chloe. "Thank you so much for helping me, both of you!"

"I can't imagine anyone wanting to hurt you, Mina," Hanna said warmly. "Everyone likes you too much."

Mina blushed. "Well, I'm just happy that we're going to the pageant after all," she said. "But we'd better hurry up, or we'll be late!"

"I'll fetch my saddlecloth," Hanna said. "We can all get ready together!"

Mina fetched her grooming kit so she and Chloe could comb Flame's and Flicker's manes and tails. Hanna came back with Ebony, and they oiled the ponies' hooves and checked their saddlecloths to make sure they were straight.

"I think we're done," Mina said, giving Flicker a final pat.

Suddenly Flame whinnied. "You've forgotten something, Chloe!" she said.

Chloe thought for a second. "The ribbons!" she cried. She ran into the tack room to fetch the bag of ribbons. There were lots of different colors, and she laid them out to see which would suit each pony.

"Blue and yellow for Flicker," she decided. "Red and gold for Flame." She looked at Ebony, whose saddlecloth was a lovely olive green with silver tassels. "And silver ribbons for Ebony!"

Chloe had never braided manes so fast in all her life, but she concentrated hard, weaving the ribbons in as she went.

"Our ponies have never looked so beautiful," Hanna declared. "Thank you, Chloe!"

The pageant took place just outside the town. As the three girls rode through the streets, Mina told Chloe about the races that took place each year.

"Everyone who has a pony joins in the pageant before the start of the races," she explained. "It's really good fun. Everyone who doesn't have a pony comes along to watch! Once the pageant is

over, there are lots of exciting races. The fastest horses from all over the desert join in."

Chloe felt her stomach flip over in excitement.

The girls made their way to the starting point for the pageant. Chloe sat up tall with her back straight, remembering all Flame's lessons. She felt confident enough to look around at all the other ponies. They had pretty dished faces, just like Flame's, and they all had spectacular saddlecloths and bridles. Some of the riders wore flowing fabric headdresses over their long embroidered gowns.

Chloe noticed that one man was walking around, looking closely at the riders. Then he stopped to talk to another man. They looked up and pointed straight at Chloe and her friends.

"Those men seem to be talking about us," Chloe said to Mina and Hanna.

"He's coming our way!" whinnied Flame, as one of the men came over.

"Hello there!" he called. "You have the prettiest ponies here. Would you like to lead the procession?"

"Lead the procession?" Mina exclaimed. She looked at Chloe and Hanna, who both grinned in delight. "We'd *love* to!"

The man showed them where to stand. "Let the pageant begin!" he called. Chloe nudged her heels against Flame's side, and the palomino walked forward with her neck proudly arched and her ears pricked. Flicker and Ebony walked beside her, looking just as beautiful. The route was lined with people, and a huge cheer went up as they trotted past.

"I can't believe it," Chloe murmured.

Flame tossed her head. "Oh, *I* can," she said. "You've made us look magnificent."

Chloe beamed until her cheeks ached. She felt as if she was going to burst with pride!

As they reached the end of the procession, Chloe gazed around at the colorful scene. Not far off, the golden sand dunes looked mysterious and inviting. Chloe longed to explore them. She looked at Mina and Hanna. They were surrounded by their friends who were congratulating them. She caught Mina's eye, and gave a little wave. As Mina waved back, Hanna turned and saw her, too, so Chloe smiled at them both.

Quickly she trotted Flame away from the crowds. As they drew near the dunes, a gust of wind lifted little eddies of sand that swirled around Flame's hooves. Chloe noticed that the sand was beginning to shimmer and the swirls were turning pink and glittery. . . .

"I think it's time for us to go," said Flame.

Chloe gazed around at the desert one last

time. She wanted to remember this adventure forever.

Flame speeded up until she was galloping over the sand, but Chloe didn't need to hang on to her mane now. Flame had helped her become a much better rider, and she felt a lot braver.

The last of the sparkles disappeared, and Chloe looked down. Instead of a real golden mane, she saw a glossy wooden neck. Flame was a carousel pony again, rising and falling smoothly as the carousel slowed to a halt. Chloe's blue cotton robe had vanished, and she was wearing her cardigan and her denim skirt again.

Chloe leaned forward and stroked Flame's neck. They had shared an amazing adventure!

"Hey, Chloe! Did you enjoy your ride?"

It was Chloe's dad, waving at her from the steps that led up to the carousel.

Chloe waved back and slid down from the saddle.

"Good-bye, Flame," she whispered, patting her golden neck.

As she turned to go, she noticed something poking out of the pocket of her pink cardigan. "That's funny!" she said. She put her hand into her pocket.

With a gasp of delight, she pulled out two of the ribbons that the stall owner had given her—a red and a gold one, entwined prettily together.

"Now I'll definitely remember my adventure forever!" She laughed.

She glanced back at Flame one last time, and was sure she could see a twinkle in her lovely brown eyes.

Chapter One

Emily was so excited, she could hardly breathe. The fairground was filled with colors and sounds, and she couldn't wait to try some of the fantastic rides. She turned slowly on the spot, wondering which ride to go on first.

"Come on, Emily! Max has spotted an airplane ride." Emily's big sister, Jane, was calling her. Jane had brought Emily and Max to the fair as a treat. They'd been looking forward to it for ages.

"Coming!" Emily called back, running after her sister. The airplanes didn't look very exciting to her, but maybe that was because she was eight and Max was only five. Jane helped Max into one of the blue and yellow planes. As the ride swooped around he made "neeeoow" noises and pretended to talk to the control tower. He was very disappointed when it stopped, so Emily suggested getting some cotton candy.

"I don't want any cotton candy!" Max wailed. "I want to go on the airplanes again!"

"But this is the only ride we've seen! The others will be fun, too," Emily promised.

"Noooo! This one, this one, this one!" Max's face turned bright red as he got ready to have one of his tantrums.

"Okay!" Jane said. "You can have one more

ride on the plane. Just one, remember!"

Max beamed, and Emily sighed. Max always got his own way because he was the youngest. She had a feeling that just one more ride wouldn't be enough for her little brother.

Luckily Max felt so dizzy after his second spin on the airplane that he didn't protest when Emily and Jane said they wanted to find some different rides.

Emily led the way through the fairground, holding one of Max's sticky hands. What should she go on? The superslide? The bumper cars?

Suddenly she heard a lovely tune playing in the distance. It was almost as if the music was calling her! She pulled Max and Jane along behind her as she followed the tinkling notes.

"Oh look!" Emily gasped.

The music was coming from an old-fashioned carousel, painted in sparkling red and gold. The colors flashed as it twirled merrily around. Emily thought she'd never seen anything so beautiful.

All three of them stopped. "It's so pretty!" said Emily. "Jane, please may I have a ride on that?"

Jane laughed. "Of course you can."

The carousel slowed down and the music faded away. Emily ran over to have a proper look at the ponies. She admired a lovely dapple-gray circus pony with twinkling eyes and a dashing Arabian with a flowing mane. Then she spotted a gorgeous pony the color of caramel ice cream that she recognized from her pony magazines. It was a snow rescue pony! Snow rescue ponies were used in mountain countries for traveling in deep snow. They were Emily's favorite kind of pony! They looked different from other ponies, with their small bodies. She loved the way they had a cute black stripe running from the top of their head all the way down their back.

The wooden pony had a kind face. Emily climbed the steps to the carousel and stroked the pony's neck. His leather bridle had little silver bells jingling on it, tied with bunches of yellow ribbon. His coat looked soft and furry—Emily knew it had to be very thick to keep him warm through snowy winters. She ran her hand down the pony's mane. It stood straight up, just like a zebra's. She noticed he had faint zebra stripes on his legs, too.

A booming voice behind Emily startled her. "Hello there! Are you admiring my mountain pony?"

Emily turned around to find a sparkly-eyed gentleman in a green velvet suit standing beside the carousel. "He's beautiful!" Emily said, running down the steps to stand beside him.

The carousel owner raised his green-striped top hat to Emily and bowed low. "I'm Mr.

Barker and this is my Magic Pony Carousel. Would you like to have a ride on one of my ponies?" he asked.

Emily nodded. "Yes, please!"

Mr. Barker rubbed his hands together, then blew on them hard. "Brrrr! It's chilly today, don't you think? Winter's on its way." He opened his hands again, revealing a little pile of pink tickets cupped in his palms.

Emily stared in astonishment. Where had all those pink tickets come from?

"Take a ticket, my dear!" said Mr Barker. "The name of your pony will be written on it."

Emily reached for the corner of a pink ticket that was poking out from the pile. She really wanted to ride the snow rescue pony! She unfolded the ticket with trembling fingers. In swirly black writing it read *Crystal*.

She looked hopefully up at Mr. Barker, and he

nodded at the carousel. "Take a look!" he said.

Emily climbed up onto the carousel again. All the ponies had a little name plate attached to the pole in front of their saddles. She peered up to read the caramel-colored pony's name. *Crystal*! It was the perfect name for a snow pony!

"Thank you!" she said to Mr. Barker. "He's exactly the pony I wanted to ride!"

Mr. Barker smiled, and Emily scrambled onto Crystal's back. His saddle was made of heavy leather. Underneath it was a beautiful dark red saddlecloth, embroidered with tiny flowers and leaves in twinkling gold thread. Emily felt so safe on Crystal's back.

Mr. Barker stood in the middle of the carousel and twirled a golden handle. The tinkling tune played once more, and Emily laughed out loud as she felt Crystal swoop into the air. She waved to Jane and Max who were watching her, and they waved back.

The carousel began to spin faster, and the fairground became a blur of laughing faces. Everything started to disappear in a rainbow mist. Emily blinked. She wanted to rub her eyes, but they were going so fast, she didn't dare let go of Crystal's reins. Silvery sparkles whirled around her, and the rainbow colors of the fairground changed to dazzling white. Everything shone and glittered with light, and Emily gasped out loud.

This wasn't the fairground anymore. She and Crystal were in the middle of a snowstorm!

Take a ride on the Magic Pony Carousel!

Magic Pony Carousel
Sparkle
1
THE CIRCUS PONY

Magic Pony Carousel
Brightheart
2
THE KNIGHT'S PONY

Magic Pony Carousel
Star
3
THE WESTERN PONY

Magic Pony Carousel
Jewel
4
THE MIDNIGHT PONY

Visit www.harpercollinschildrens.com
to decorate your own Magic Pony!